THE DRAGON PACK SNACK ATTACK

FASTFUDEM

BURGERHUTIUM

story by Joel E. Tanis *and* Jeff Grooters

pictures by Joel E. Tanis

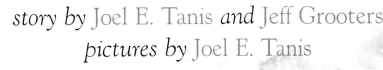

Four Winds Press ❖ *New York*

Maxwell Macmillan Canada *Toronto* Maxwell Macmillan International *New York* Oxford Singapore Sydney

Hi, I'm Spittleshnazz... and I wouldn't want to eat any applesauce that Cuddlefluff just sat on.

Hi, I'm Roofus. I enjoy oceanic breezes, wild flowers, and horseback riding ... I mean riders.

Hi, I'm Cuddlefluff
I weigh 1,700 pounds.
If I sit on a bushel of apples,
I can make applesauce.

Four Winds Press
Macmillan Publishing Company
866 Third Avenue
New York, NY 10022

Maxwell Macmillan Canada, Inc.
1200 Eglinton Avenue East
Suite 200
Don Mills, Ontario M3C 3N1

Macmillan Publishing Company is part of
the Maxwell Communication Group of Companies.

First edition
Printed and bound in Singapore.
10 9 8 7 6 5 4 3 2 1

The text of this book is set in Kennerly Oldstyle.
The illustrations are rendered in watercolor.
Typography by Christy Hale

Library of Congress Cataloging-in-Publication Data
Tanis, Joel E.
The dragon pack snack attack / story by Joel E. Tanis and Jeff Grooters ;
pictures by Joel E. Tanis. — 1st ed.
p.   cm.
Summary: After spending hundreds of years on a tropical island,
a patrol of bored and hungry dragons invades civilization
and indulges in a fanatic fast food binge.
ISBN 0-02-788840-1
[1. Dragons—Fiction.   2. Food habits—Fiction.]
I. Grooters, Jeff.   II. Title.
PZ7.T1615Dr   1993
[E]—dc20   92-18433

Thank you and hello. My name is Razztatlin. I squeeze my own juice and use the leftover armor for garbage cans.

Hi, my name is Flosskin. I'm the one that posed for all of those dragon pictures on shields and crests and stuff.

To Mom, Dad, Pooh-Kitty, and Jesus.
Not necessarily in that order.

—Joel

I'm Hobart. This is boring. Let's start the story.

To my mom, who had me, and my dad, who let her keep me.
To my family, who are the bones of my soul.

—Jeff

Once upon a time, huge dragons roamed the earth. In fact, they did a lot more than just roam it. They did a pretty darn good job of terrorizing it, too. I'm sure you've heard how it was. . . . Dragons were famous for swiping gold, bashing knights, and breathing fire on pretty much whatever they felt like breathing fire on.

Terrorizing was fun for a few hundred years, but after a while it got *boring*. Hobart, an *especially* bored dragon, decided he needed a vacation.

"Time to hit the beach!" he declared, which is just the sort of thing you'd expect a dragon to say if he was going on vacation. "After all," Hobart said, "the good gold is gone . . . most of the knights have been beaten and eaten . . . and fire-breathing just gives *me* a stomachache."

And off he flew.

The other dragons were weary with dragon shenanigans, too. So a day or two later, they *all* went to the beach. . . .

Well, basking in the sun was

pretty perfect
for fifty years,

nifty for another fifty,

really relaxing
for a hundred,

halfway happy
for another fifty,

maybe mediocre
for yet another hundred,

then finally not so nifty for a really long, laborious fifty.
Hobart was bored again. He was not only bored,
he was feeling a little hungry, too.

"I've got the munchies. Let's get out of here!" exclaimed Hobart to his friends, which is just what you'd expect from a bored, hungry dragon. And with that, they all flew off to find something juicy for a late-afternoon snack.

The first possible snack the dragons came across was a brawny guy leaning against a wall.

Razztatlin was somewhat in favor of eating him, but he finally said, "He can't be all *that* juicy."

Hobart said, "No tough guys! We can find something less chewy."

The others agreed, and so they moved on.

The little kid in the park looked okay to Cuddlefluff, but dragons don't like sweets, and most little kids are just too sugary.

"She does look pretty juicy, though," Cuddlefluff observed.

"There must be *something* better to snack on than people," Hobart pointed out.

So once again, the dragons moved on.

Then *it* happened. Hobart smelled something wonderful. A savory smell unlike anything he had ever sniffed or snarfed before. "Super! It's suppertime!" cried Hobart.

"Follow that smell!" cheered Razztatlin.

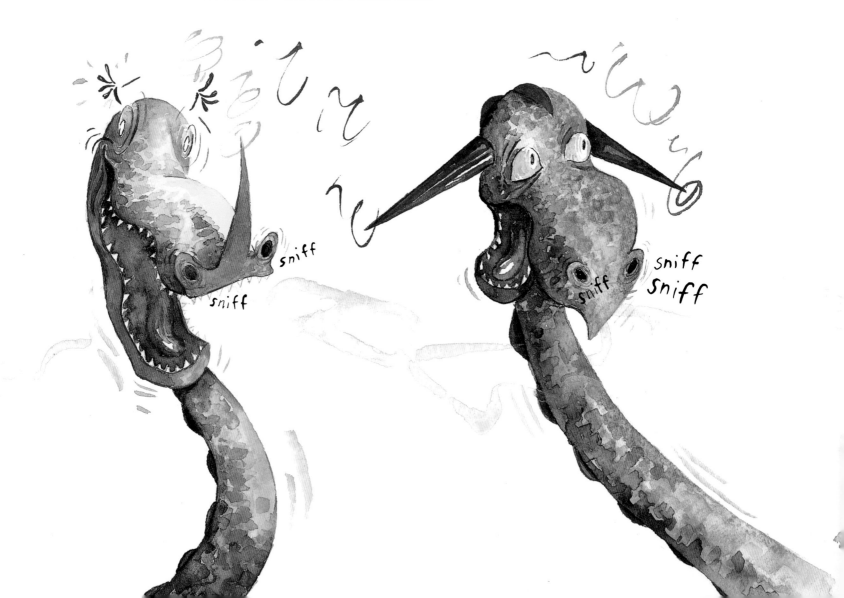

And the dragons followed their noses to the source of the amazing aroma. . . .

Burger Hut!

It did not take long for Hobart's stomach to tell him what to do.
The other dragons watched with eager eyes as Hobart strolled up to
the drive-through window. In his most pleasant dragon voice, he said,
"Yes, I'll take a thousand of everything, please," which is just the sort
of thing you'd expect a hungry dragon to say.

The owner, Mr. Melon, had never seen a dragon before, and was never really expecting to see one. But Friendly and Speedy Service was his motto. Recognizing that Hobart was from out of town, he said, "But, sir, a thousand of everything would cost a fortune."

"Will *this* fortune do?" replied Hobart.

"Well, fortunately, I am accepting piles of gold today," beamed Mr. Melon.

Life was good for the dragons. You could often hear them say things like:

"Throw me another Hutburger!"

"Yes, I'll take a thousand of everything, please."

"*Yum, yum, smack, smack, yum.*"

Life was good for Mr. Melon, too. You could often hear him say things like:
"One thousand, two thousand, three thousand . . ."

Burger Hut

DRAGONS WELCOME

Hobart and his friends loved Burger Hut! In fact, you could say that the dragons were having a full-blown, fantastic, fanatic food festival!

"Dragons are graceful, glorious, and good," said Mr. Melon.

But alas, only three weeks later, the dragons ran out of gold!

"Dragons are filthy, foul, and foolish," was Mr. Melon's new cry. "No more Hutburgers for them!"

Hobart and his friends did not know what to do.

They loved Hutburgers! They *lived* for Hutburgers!

After careful thought, Hobart devised a plan.

He ran to the nearest telephone. . . . "Yes, I'd like to have some food delivered. . . . A thousand of everything, please."

But, to his dismay, the voice on the other end of the line responded, "Forget it, Hobart, I know that's you. Only dragons order a thousand of everything."

"Well, okay then, how about ten of each?" Hobart tried.

"Hobart, you can't trick me," a mad Mr. Melon replied.

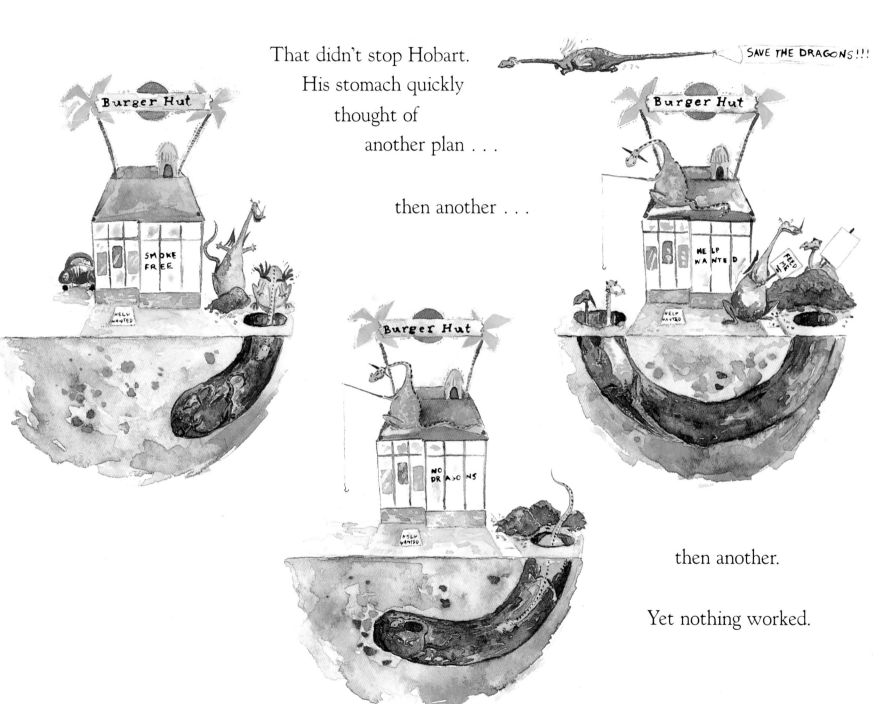

That didn't stop Hobart.
His stomach quickly
thought of
another plan . . .

then another . . .

then another.

Yet nothing worked.

Then Hobart came up with the perfect idea. He thought the dragons could dress up like people, order the food, then grab it and run.

But, for some reason, Mr. Melon saw through their disguises. "Get out of here, you crafty creatures!" he bellowed.

"What do you mean? Can't you see we're people?" argued Roofus.

Mr. Melon would not budge.

Now the dragons were beginning to get desperate. They even tried picking up the cars in the Burger Hut parking lot and shaking them until the food fell out.

The dragons were out of ideas and out of luck.
The situation was getting worse and worse, not only for the hungry dragons, but for Mr. Melon, too. All of his customers were scared away.

Then a merry Mr. Melon had the *ideal* idea! He directed the dragons to the sign in front of Burger Hut: HELP WANTED it said.

"I should have thought of that!" said Hobart. "Then again, I never had a job before."

"Unless you count frying knights," Spittleshnazz sputtered.

Well, soon the dragons were *frying hamburgers!*

care for any fries with that?

The dragons really loved their new jobs. They cooked faster than any grill or stove. They got to snack on Hutburgers every day, all day. And with the fastest fast food ever, Mr. Melon's restaurant quickly became a huge success. In fact, he was so thankful that he changed the name from Burger Hut to Hobart Hut.

And they all lived happily ever after . . . just like you'd expect they would.